* Newly il.

# Big or Little?

WITHDRAWN

Toby

# Kathy Stinson
# Toni Goffe

annick press
toronto + new york + vancouver

We acknowledge the support of the Canada Council for the Arts, the Ontario Arts Council, and the Government of Canada through the Book Publishing Industry Development Program (BPIDP) for our publishing activities.

 ONTARIO ARTS COUNCIL
CONSEIL DES ARTS DE L'ONTARIO

**Cataloging in Publication**

Stinson, Kathy
     Big or little? / story, Kathy Stinson ; art, Toni Goffe.

"Newly illustrated 25 years".
ISBN 978-1-55451-169-3 (bound).–ISBN 978-1-55451-168-6 (pbk.)


     I. Goffe, Toni  II. Title.

PS8587.T56B5 2008           jC813'.54          C2008-905397-4


Distributed in Canada by:
Firefly Books Ltd.
66 Leek Crescent
Richmond Hill, ON
L4B 1H1

Published in the U.S.A. by:
Annick Press (U.S.) Ltd.
Distributed in the U.S.A. by:
Firefly Books (U.S.) Inc.
P.O. Box 1338
Ellicott Station
Buffalo, NY 14205


Printed in China.

Visit Annick at: www.annickpress.com
Visit the author at: www.kathystinson.com
Visit the illustrator at: www.tonigoffe.com

Sometimes
I feel
**big.**

Like when I can reach
Number 7 in the elevator.

And when I pour milk on my cereal all by myself.

But sometimes I feel little.
Like when the milk spills.

Or if I wake up and my bed's wet.

Sometimes I shave, just like my dad.
That means I'm big.

And I help my mom wash her car.
That means I'm big too.

But I still have to sit in a car seat.
That means I'm little.

Getting lost between the cereal and the cookies means I'm little too.

When I'm very big, I will drive the car
and I will never get lost.

"Thank you for holding
the door, Toby."
Only big kids hold
doors for people.

And only big kids say,
"Hi, Mr. Wong."
Big kids like me.

Yesterday I rode my bike all the way to the park. So maybe I am big now.

Except I was too scared to pat the dog at
the corner. So maybe I'm still little.

Sometimes Josh says, "Go away,"
because he thinks I'm little.

But Miss Conrad says remembering my library book every Tuesday means I'm big.

Also, I can read the words in some of my books. That means I'm really big!!

I can also print my name.

Sharing toys with my sister
means I'm big.

So does having a birthday.

Except if my aunt gives me
pajamas with bunny feet.
That means I'm little.

But hey! These bunny pajamas
don't fit me at all! I'm too big!

When I stay up late to watch basketball on TV,
that's because I'm big.

But if I fall asleep before the game is over,
and then my dad has to carry me to bed,
that's because I'm little.

Mostly I want to be big.
But sometimes I like being little too.